THUDD

Hiya! My name Thudd. Best robot friend of Drewd. Thudd know lots of stuff. How bats find bugs in dark. What make cave. Why lots of cave animals not got eyes.

Drewd like to invent stuff. Thudd help! But Drewd make lots of mistakes. Drewd invent shrinking machine. Now Drewd small as beetle. Fly into cave on back of bat. Want to see what happen? Turn page, please!

Get lost with
Andrew, Judy, and Thudd
in all their exciting adventures!

ANDREW LOST

14

WITH THE BATS

BY J. C. GREENBURG

ILLUSTRATED
BY JAN GERARDI

A STEPPING STONE BOOK™

Random House 🏠 New York

*To Dan, Zack, and the real Andrew,
with a galaxy of love.
To the children who read these books: I wish
you wonderful questions. Questions are
telescopes into the universe!*
—J.C.G.

To Cathy Goldsmith, with many thanks.
—J.G.

Text copyright © 2006 by J. C. Greenburg
Illustrations copyright © 2006 by Jan Gerardi

All rights reserved. Published in the United States by Random House Children's Books, a division of Random House, Inc., New York.

www.randomhouse.com/kids/AndrewLost
www.AndrewLost.com

Educators and librarians, for a variety of teaching tools, visit us at www.randomhouse.com/teachers

Library of Congress Cataloging-in-Publication Data
Greenburg, J. C. (Judith C.)
With the bats / by J. C. Greenburg ; illustrated by Jan Gerardi.
    p.   cm. — (Andrew Lost ; 14)
SUMMARY: When Andrew and Judy, still the size of beetles, are carried into a cave, they learn more than they ever wanted to know about the bats and bugs that live there from Thudd the robot—and personal experience.
ISBN-10: 0-375-83563-6 (trade) — ISBN-10: 0-375-93563-0 (lib. bdg.)
ISBN-13: 978-0-375-83563-6 (trade) —
ISBN-13: 978-0-375-93563-3 (lib. bdg.)
[1. Caves—Fiction. 2. Bats—Fiction. 3. Insects—Fiction.
4. Worms—Fiction. 5. Time travel—Fiction. 6. Cousins—Fiction.]
I. Gerardi, Jan, ill. II. Title. III. Series.
PZ7.G82785Whq 2005   [Fic]—dc22   2005025617

Printed in the United States of America
10 9 8 7 6 5 4 3 2   First Edition

CONTENTS

THUDD

ANDREW'S WORLD

Andrew Dubble

Andrew is ten years old, but he's been inventing things since he was four. Andrew's inventions usually get him into trouble, like the time he invented the Aroma-Rama. It was supposed to make homes and offices smell like flowers. Instead, it made everything smell like stinky feet!

Andrew's newest invention was supposed to save the world from getting buried in garbage. Instead, it squashed Andrew and his cousin Judy down to beetle size. They got hauled off to a dump, thrown up by a sea-gull, and carried off by a bat!

Judy Dubble

Judy is Andrew's thirteen-year-old cousin. She's been snuffled into a dog's nose, pooped out of a whale, and had her pajamas chewed by a Tyrannosaurus—all because of Andrew. But after today, Judy may look back on those things as the good times!

Thudd

The **H**andy **U**ltra-**D**igital **D**etective. Thudd is a super-smart robot and Andrew's best friend. He has helped save Andrew and Judy from the exploding sun, a giant squid, and a monster asteroid. But can he keep them from drowning in bat poop or being munched by weird cave creatures?

The Goa Constrictor

This giant fake snake is Andrew's newest invention. *Goa* is sort of short for **G**arbage **Go**es **A**way. The Goa is supposed to keep the world from getting buried in garbage by squashing rotting vegetables, green meat, and dirty paper dishes down to teensy-weensy specks. Unfortunately for Andrew, the Goa doesn't just shrink garbage. In two minutes and one stinky burp, the Goa can shrink anything—and anyone!

1 GOING BATTY

"Yaaaaargh!" hollered Andrew Dubble. He was the size of a beetle and clinging to the back of a bat.

The bat zigged and zagged through the night sky. It was searching for its dinner of bugs.

The wind stung Andrew's eyes. Every zig and zag made Andrew's stomach slosh. *Urf!* he thought. *I feel like throwing up.*

URRRRRP!

Andrew popped out a garlicky burp. *It's the pepperoni pizza from lunch,* he thought. He gripped the soft fur of the bat's neck tighter.

meep . . . "Drewd okey-dokey?" came a squeaky voice from Andrew's shirt pocket.

It was Thudd, Andrew's little silver robot and best friend.

"It's like the worst roller-coaster ride," said Andrew. "And there's no safety belt!"

"Androooooooo!" came a wail from the other side of the bat.

Light from the full moon lit the frowning face of Judy Dubble, Andrew's thirteen-year-old cousin. She was dangling from the tip of one of the bat's big ears.

Like Andrew, Judy had been shrunk as small as a beetle by Andrew's latest invention, the Goa Constrictor. *Goa* was sort of short for **G**arbage **Go**es **A**way. Andrew's invention was supposed to squash garbage atoms. It turns out the Goa could squash the atoms of anything—or anyone!

"Jooodeeeeee!" hollered Andrew over the wind. "Get onto the back of the bat!

You won't flap around so much!"

"Whaaaat?" yelled Judy. "I can't hear you! I'm trying to get off this stupid ear!"

Judy reached down and grabbed a fistful of fur on the bat's neck. Then she let go of the ear.

The wind caught her and bounced her on the bat's neck. With her free hand waving through the air, Judy looked like a cowgirl at a rodeo.

Finally, Judy managed to grab on to the bat's neck with both hands. She tucked herself behind the bat's ear.

The air around the bat was swarming with specks and dots. Andrew recognized the ones that came close—they were mosquitoes, beetles, and moths.

Nyeeeeeee . . .

A high-pitched whine whistled in Andrew's ears.

meep . . . "Mosquito!" said Thudd.

Nyeee—

The sound suddenly stopped. The bat had scooped the annoying insect into its wide-open mouth.

"Wowzers!" said Andrew. "This bat can catch an awfully fast bug! I could barely see it!"

meep . . . "Bat not use eyes to find bug," said Thudd. "Bat send out sound. Sound bounce off bug. Like echo. Sound bounce back to bat ears."

Thudd pointed to his face screen.

eck-oh-loh-KAY-shun

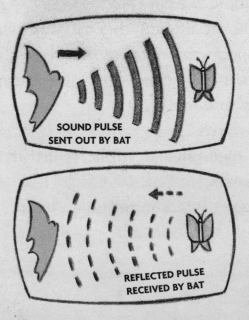

SOUND PULSE
SENT OUT BY BAT

REFLECTED PULSE
RECEIVED BY BAT

"Bat brain figure out 'xactly where bug is. Called echolocation. Use echo to find bugs to eat.

"This bat eat three thousand bugs every night!" Thudd continued. "Bat can eat as much as bat weigh!"

"Holy moly!" said Andrew. "That would be like me eating eighty pounds of pizza!"

Judy was shaking her head. "I don't know, Thudd. I don't hear the bat making any bug-finding sounds."

meep . . . "Bat sound too high for human to hear," said Thudd.

"Like whale sounds are too low for us to hear," said Andrew.

"Yoop! Yoop! Yoop!" said Thudd.

Suddenly the moon went dark.

Andrew looked up. A huge shape with horns and wings was blotting it out!

Eek! "Great horned owl!" squeaked Thudd. "Great horned owl eat bats!"

"And *us*!" said Judy.

SPACE ALIENS?

"We'll end up as owl pellets!" Judy moaned.

"Huh?" said Andrew.

"Little balls of hair and bones that owls throw up after dinner!" said Judy.

"It's pretty dark," said Andrew. "Maybe the owl won't see us."

meep . . . "Owl got great eyes to see at night," said Thudd. "Can see mouse two football fields away. And full moon help owl eyes."

"We don't have a chance!" said Judy.

meep . . . "Bat got one chance, maybe," said Thudd. "Bat move wings more ways than owl. Bat zigzag fast, fast, fast! Hard for owl to follow."

"But I don't think the bat sees the owl!" said Andrew.

Andrew glanced over his shoulder. The owl swooped closer. Its two coal-red eyes glowed in its horned head.

"Thudd," said Judy. "What's this bat's favorite food?"

meep . . . "Moth!" squeaked Thudd.

"Andrew!" said Judy. "Grab the sleeve of my jacket and pull!"

Andrew helped Judy wriggle out of her jacket. Then she tossed it high into the air.

"Maybe the bat will think my jacket's a moth," said Judy. "If I threw it right, maybe the bat will see the owl. It's our only chance."

The bat zoomed up toward the jacket. Suddenly it swerved. It dove through the night in a dizzying twist.

"I think the bat saw the owl!" said Judy.

Andrew could barely hang on. They were headed straight toward something big and dark.

This bat's about to crash! he thought.

The next second, Andrew almost flew off the bat as it jerked to a stop.

They had landed on the scaly bark of a tree trunk. The bat folded itself like a paper origami bird. Then it squeezed into a crack in the bark as small as a dime.

Graaaaaak . . . graaaaaak . . .

The owl had landed on the tree. It was tearing at the bark with its beak.

The bat folded itself even more tightly and squeezed deeper into the crack.

"Ugh!" groaned Judy. "Now I'm getting smooshed!"

"Better than getting turned into an owl pellet," said Andrew.

The beak pulled away, and Andrew heard a soft flapping of wings.

meep . . . "Owl give up!" said Thudd. "Hunt other prey." The bat crept out of the crack. Using a claw in the middle of each wing, it pulled itself up the tree trunk.

meep . . . "Bat wing like hand with long, long fingers," said Thudd. "Fingers covered

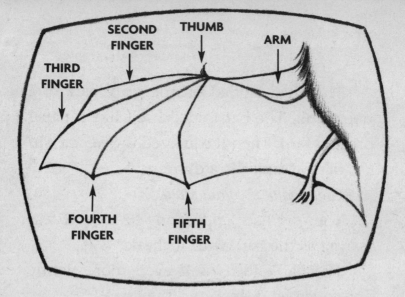

with skin. Claw on bat wing is bat thumb."

The bat crept out to a tree branch and hung upside down by its feet. Then it spread its wings and let go.

It dipped and swirled through the tangled branches of a forest.

"How long is this bat gonna stay out?" asked Judy.

meep . . . "Bat stay out till dawn," said Thudd. "Unless bat is mother bat. Mother bat go back to feed baby bat many times in night."

Judy buried her face in the bat's fur and

shook her head. "I can't hang on to this stupid bat for eight hours!" she moaned. "I sure hope this bat's got a kid."

meep . . . "Baby bat called pup," said Thudd.

"I sure do feel yucky," said Andrew. He gave another loud, garlic-flavored burp.

Below them, Andrew saw the reflection of the moon.

We're flying over water, he thought.

"Yaaaaaah!" hollered Judy, looking down. "What's *that*?"

Floating a few feet above the water was a glowing ball of yellow-green light. As they watched, another ball of light appeared.

The glowing balls grew brighter and dimmer, brighter and dimmer. They throbbed like a heartbeat.

Suddenly they rose like hot-air balloons!

Andrew could feel his heart beating faster. *Could it be?* he wondered. *Could it really be . . . space aliens?*

3

KEEEK! KEEEK! ACK!

"Looks like ghosts!" said Judy.

The bat flew close to one of the spooky balls. Insects were swirling around it.

"I can see right through it!" said Andrew.

meep . . . "Swamp lights!" said Thudd. "Sometimes called foxfire. Sometimes called, um, swamp farts."

Andrew laughed. Judy rolled her eyes.

meep . . . "Lotsa dead stuff collect under swamp water," said Thudd. "Bacteria eat dead stuff. Burp up stuff called swamp gas. Swamp gas make big bubble. Bubble pop up to top of water. Swamp gas catch fire! Make light!

"Swamp gas come from dumps and land-fills, too," Thudd added. "Sometimes humans collect swamp gas. Use to cook. Make heat for house."

Andrew watched the bat scoop up mouth-fuls of insects.

"There are so many bugs around the light!" said Andrew.

meep . . . "Lotsa bugs fly to light," said Thudd. "Nobody sure why. Maybe it's cuz bugs think light is moon. Lotsa bugs use moon like map. Help bug fly in right direc-tion."

The bat flitted away from the bouncing, flickering lights. Ahead, the sharp peak of a mountain clawed the moonlit sky.

The bat was flying straight now. It wasn't hunting. Andrew could see other bats head-ing in the same direction.

"I think our bat is going home," said Andrew.

"Oh, *great*," said Judy. "We'll end up in a disgusting cave where we'll get eaten by snakes or lizards or giant spiders. Maybe there are *vampire bats* in there!"

"Oh, come on," said Andrew. "We got back from the beginning of the universe, we can get out of a cave."

meep . . . "Oody not have to worry about vampire bat," squeaked Thudd. "Vampire bat live in South America."

As the bat flew closer to the mountain, Andrew saw a jagged crack near the bottom. *That must be an entrance to the cave,* thought Andrew.

The bat swooshed through the crack into deep darkness.

ch-ch-ch . . . *caw* . . . *thwerp-thwerp* . . . *ka-ka-ka* . . .

Andrew couldn't see a thing, but he could hear the chattering, buzzing, and clicking of bats.

"What a racket!" said Judy. "I thought bats made sounds we can't hear."

meep . . . "Bat use super-high sounds for hunting," said Thudd. "Bat talk to other bat with sound humans can hear."

Their bat was slowing down.

meep . . . "Bat gonna land on ceiling," Thudd squeaked. "Gotta fly slow, slow, slow. Then use foot claws or thumb claws to grab on to ceiling of cave."

For a second, the bat seemed to stop flying. Suddenly Andrew felt himself flipping over!

"YEOW!" he hollered. "Hang on, Thudd!"

"Yaaaaaaah!" screamed Judy.

The bat had landed. It was hanging from the ceiling by its feet.

Andrew was struggling to keep his grip on the bat's fur as he dangled in the darkness.

The bat swung forward, grabbed on to the ceiling with the claws on its wings, and began creeping along.

Eeek-eeek . . . *kuh-kuh-kuh,* their bat squawked.

meep . . . "This bat is mom bat," said Thudd. "Look for baby bat by sound, by smell. Mom make sound, baby answer. Every baby smell different."

"Babies smell stinky," said Judy. "*Erg!* I can't hang on much longer. I'm gonna try to get under her wing. *Ooomph!*"

"Me too," said Andrew.

After Andrew climbed under the wing, he unhooked his mini-flashlight from his belt and shoved the back of it against his forehead. He had fitted it with a suction cup. That way, he could see and use both hands.

He turned on the flashlight.

"Wowzers schnauzers!" cried Andrew.

As far as he could see, every inch of the cave ceiling was crawling with tiny, noisy bat babies.

"There must be thousands of bats here!" said Andrew.

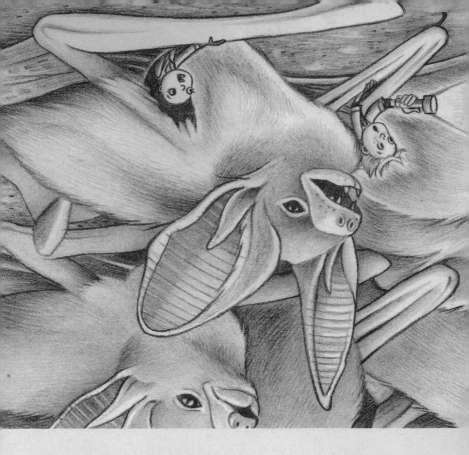

meep . . . "Maybe millions," said Thudd.

"Too many," said Judy.

Chirping and squeaking, their bat crept across the crowded ceiling like a fly.

Now and then, she'd stop to sniff a pup.

Keeek! Keeek! Ack! chirped a baby bat nearby.

Their bat stopped to sniff it. This time she let go of the ceiling with her thumb claws and hung upside down by her feet.

Then she opened her wings.

"YIKES!" cried Judy, clinging to the leathery edge of her bat wing for dear life.

"YAAAAARGH!" hollered Andrew.

The tiny, hairless pup crept toward its mother. Using its feet and wing claws, it climbed onto her chest. Then it poked its nose into her fur. She wrapped her wings snugly around her pup.

meep . . . "Baby bat drink milk from mom bat," said Thudd.

Judy sighed. "As soon as the pup finishes, she'll fly off again to eat another billion bugs. We've got to get off this bat."

Andrew thought for a moment. "The baby bat is small, but he's a lot bigger than we are," said Andrew. "We can climb onto him. When his mom leaves, we can get off of him and find a way out of this cave."

Andrew pulled himself along the edge of the mom bat's wing, then onto the fur of her chest. He reached out and touched the baby. It didn't seem to notice.

Andrew squeezed himself between the little bat and its mother. He grabbed on to the baby's wing.

"Hey, Judy!" he yelled. "We can do this! Come on!"

Slowly and carefully, Judy pulled herself toward the baby bat. With a tired groan, she tucked herself into a fold of skin under its other wing.

After a couple of minutes, the baby bat crawled off its mother and clawed its way into the pile of baby bats on the ceiling. It folded its wings. Now Andrew and Judy were tucked tightly between its wings and its body. Then it let itself hang by its feet.

The mom bat let go of the rocky ceiling,

spread her wings, and flew off.

Judy groaned. "I'm getting such a headache from being upside down. What a stupid way to live."

meep . . . "If bat not hang upside down, bat not fly," said Thudd. "Bird wing lift bird from ground. Bat wing different. Bat gotta spread wings and fall to fly."

"Look," said Andrew softly. "Our little guy is snoozing already. I wonder why bats don't let go of the ceiling when they're asleep."

meep . . . "Drewd and Oody gotta use muscles to grab stuff, hold stuff," said Thudd. "Bat feet not use muscles to hold on to stuff. When bat hang upside down, weight of bat make foot claw lock. Like hanging from hook."

Another mother bat was creeping through the crowd toward a pup nearby. The hairless little one scuttled clumsily toward her, pushing past Andrew and Judy's bat.

Suddenly they were falling. Their baby bat had gotten knocked off the ceiling!

BEETLE BATTLE

Flump . . .

Andrew's brain clunked against his skull as they hit the ground. It was a surprisingly soft landing.

They had landed on something squishy.

"Worms!" yelled Andrew.

Eek! Eeeeeek! Ack! Ack! Ack! the baby bat squawked. It began to creep along the floor of the cave.

Andrew and Judy climbed atop the bat's wings.

"*Euuuw!*" said Judy. "Smells like someone didn't clean the litter box—*ever!*"

meep . . . "Bat poop!" said Thudd. "Called

guano. Very stinky stuff. Super stinky!"

As the baby bat scuttled along, Andrew's flashlight beam lit the floor of the cave.

White worms tangled in twisting knots. Beetles were scrambling over the worms.

"I don't see any poop," said Andrew. "Just zillions of worms and bugs."

meep . . . "Poop underneath wormy guys," said Thudd.

Ploop . . .

A big, dark, sticky drop splashed down in front of the baby bat.

Plooorp . . . *plooomp* . . .

More drops were falling around them. It sounded a lot like a slow rain.

meep . . . "*Now* Drewd see bat poop," said Thudd.

"*Eeeeeuuuw!*" groaned Judy.

meep . . . "Bats poop here thousand years, maybe more," said Thudd. "Make lotsa, lotsa poop."

Judy's face scrunched up. "*Yuck-a-roony!*

Don't make me come over there and take out your batteries, Thudd," she said.

meep . . . "Bat poop is good stuff, Oody," said Thudd. "Is food for lotsa animals in cave. Like little wormy guys. Wormy guys eat bat poop like candy!"

A streak of bright green light zigzagged toward the baby bat. It was a centipede. And it was battling three giant beetles!

meep . . . "When this centipede scared, it make glow-in-dark color," said Thudd.

The centipede and beetles tumbled toward them. The centipede flung the beetles onto the baby bat's wings!

Eeeek! squeaked Thudd. "This kinda beetle eat living animals!"

Eeek! Ack! Eeeeeek! the baby bat squeaked loudly.

"We can't let them hurt the baby!" said Judy.

She crawled over the baby bat's wing and punched one of the beetles between its eyes.

"Take *that*!" she yelled. Then she grabbed the beetle by its antennas and tossed it off the baby bat. But the beetle was heavy. Judy lost her balance and fell off the bat's wing!

Andrew tugged the flashlight off his forehead and whacked another beetle on the head. But that just seemed to make it angry.

It charged at Andrew. It shoved him off the wing and onto the squishy worms below. Then it opened its scissor-like jaws and reached for Andrew's neck!

meep . . . "Breathe on beetle!" squeaked Thudd. "Drewd got garlic breath. Beetle hate garlic!"

Andrew huffed and puffed as hard as he could at the beetle. It backed away! Another beetle came up behind Andrew. Andrew turned and blew at that one, too. He blew so hard, he felt dizzy.

Andrew heard soft flapping above him.

The next instant, he saw a big bat swooping down. It plucked the baby from the

ground with its clawed feet and zoomed toward the ceiling of the cave.

meep . . . "Bats help bats," said Thudd. "Big
bats help baby bats. Healthy bats help sick bats."

"Ooooof!" Andrew heard Judy yelling
nearby. "That's what you get for trying to eat
me! Now get out of here!"

"What are you doing?" hollered Andrew.

"Beating this ugly bug's butt!" Judy yelled
back.

Andrew was swimming in an ocean of squirmy, wormy creatures. Their slimy little bodies rubbed against Andrew's legs.

"It's like walking through a field of wiggly sausages," said Andrew.

"Andrew!" yelled Judy. "Watch out behind you!"

Andrew turned to see a wide, flat, armored creature scurrying straight at him. Compared to Andrew, it was as big as a tank.

"Woofers!" hollered Andrew, leaping over worms.

The creature was faster than Andrew. It shoved him facedown into the wriggling sea of baby beetles.

meep . . . "Giant cave cockroach!" squeaked Thudd.

Andrew pulled himself up and wiped slime off his face. He looked up to see Judy standing over him. She was still catching her breath from her bug battle.

"Okay, Disaster Master," she said. "How are we going to get out of here without being eaten by bugs or something worse?"

meep . . . "Drewd! Look!" squeaked Thudd from Andrew's pocket. He was pointing to a strange white shape. It looked like the monster roach they had just seen. But it was upside down with its legs in the air.

"Looks like a dead one," said Judy.

"Noop! Noop! Noop!" said Thudd. "Empty skeleton of roach.

"All bugs got skeleton on outside. Called exoskeleton. *Exo* mean 'outside.'

"Bug grow. Bug skeleton not grow. When bug get too big for skeleton, skeleton split. Come off. Bug got new skeleton underneath. But new skeleton soft. In few hours, bug skeleton get hard.

"Bug skeleton help Drewd and Oody! Use like armor!"

"Come on, Judy," said Andrew. "Let's take a look."

Andrew shoved his way through the wormy sea toward the bug skeleton. Judy rolled her eyes and followed him.

Andrew reached the skeleton. His flashlight shined through it like thin paper. He poked it.

"Feels like hard plastic," he said. "And it's big enough to cover both of us."

Andrew stuck his flashlight back onto his head and pushed the skeleton onto its side. It felt light. "There's a big slit on the back of it!" he said.

meep . . . "When bug get too big for skeleton, skeleton crack," said Thudd.

"Get under here, Judy!" said Andrew.

"And then what?" Judy asked.

"And then you might not get eaten by that
big weird thing behind you!" said Andrew.

5 UH-OH, GUANO!

Andrew's light shined on a snakey head with frills on the sides. The creature's body was snakey, too, but it had four legs. Its skin was white and so thin that they could see its insides!

"Cheese Louise!" Judy shouted. She scrambled under the roach skeleton with Andrew.

It wasn't quite high enough for them to stand up, so they had to crouch, waist-deep, among the slimy, wriggling worms.

meep . . . "Blind cave salamander!" said Thudd.

"Whew!" sighed Judy. "If it's blind, it can't find us."

"Noop! Noop! Noop!" said Thudd. "Cave salamander smell stuff. Feel stuff move. Find what move. Eat what move."

The bug skeleton shook. They could see a blurry shadow through the skeleton. It was the salamander's head wagging above them.

"It's gonna get us!" cried Judy.

Andrew felt a poke from Thudd in his pocket.

meep . . . "Cave salamander not like heat," said Thudd. "Flashlight make heat. Drewd gotta shine light on salamander head. Hurry!"

Andrew lifted the skeleton a crack. The spooky white head was a quarter-inch away.

Andrew shined his flashlight beam right in the salamander's face. It reared its head, then turned and scooted into the darkness.

meep . . . "Salamander need to be wet, need to be in water," said Thudd. "Follow salamander, get to water. Find way to get out, maybe."

Judy rolled her eyes. "How is water going to get us out of here?" she asked.

meep . . . "Cave made by water," said Thudd. "Water come into cave. Water come out someplace. Find stream, find river in cave, find way out of cave."

"Follow that salamander!" said Andrew.

With Andrew in front of Judy, they balanced the bug skeleton on their heads. The light on Andrew's forehead shined through the skeleton just enough for them to see where they were going.

Slowly, they began plodding along in the direction the salamander had taken. With every step, they had to plow their way through slimy, wormy things.

In places with fewer worms, their feet sank ankle-deep into bat guano.

"Gross-a-mundo!" complained Judy. "This is soooo disgusting!"

"Feels like sloshing through mud," said Andrew.

As they pushed on and on, the cries of the bats sounded farther away. Fewer squishy things rubbed against them. Soon they were scratching their legs on sharp pebbles and rocks, not sinking into bat poop.

The air felt cool and damp against Andrew's skin. The farther they went, the colder it got.

"I haven't had to smack a stupid bug for at least half an hour," said Judy. "Let's get out of this creepy shell. It's giving me a headache."

"I guess we could do that," said Andrew. "It'll be easier to see where we're going. One, two, three, push!"

The bug skeleton tumbled onto its side.

Andrew squinted. Was that a dim glow in the distance or was he imagining it? He rubbed his eyes. The glow was still there.

"I see light!" he shouted.

BACK TO THE STONE AGE

"I see it, too!" said Judy. "Maybe it's a way out of here. Move it, Bug-Brain!"

Thudd's jellybean-shaped feet were kicking in Andrew's pocket.

meep . . . "Drewd! Take exoskeleton!" said Thudd. "Might need later. Cave is dangerous place."

Andrew and Judy picked up the bug skeleton and carried it between them.

As they hurried toward the glow, they came to a place where the rock floor was smooth and flat. A curved wall blocked the way ahead of them.

The wall was yellowish white and smooth. It was several inches high and towered over them.

Andrew touched it. "This reminds me of something," he said.

meep . . . "Mammoth tusk!" said Thudd.

"Jeepers creepers!" Andrew whispered. He thought of Max the mammoth from their adventure in the Ice Age 14,000 years ago.

Andrew shined his light on the ground near the base of the tusk. There was a small crack of space. "Let's go through here," Andrew said.

Andrew and Judy shoved the bug skeleton ahead of them, then slipped through themselves.

On the other side of the tusk, their feet stirred up little clouds of dark dust.

Andrew beamed his light around. They were in a circle made of mammoth tusks!

"Wowzers schnauzers!" said Andrew.

"Someone *made* this circle!"

As they trekked across the circle, they passed lumpy chunks that towered over them like black hills.

"Wait a minute," said Andrew. He put down the bug skeleton and rubbed one of the chunks. It made his hand black.

"This feels like charcoal," he said. "The black dust we're kicking up is soot. Someone made a fire here!"

meep . . . "Thousands, thousands of years ago, people use cave as home," said Thudd. "Cook food. Sleep. Hide from bear. Hide from saber-tooth tiger. But sometime tiger and bear live in cave, too."

Andrew walked around a flat stone. It had sharp chipped edges and a point at one end.

"It's an arrowhead!" said Andrew.

"Yoop! Yoop! Yoop!" said Thudd. "This time called Stone Age cuz people make tools from stone.

"See two stones next to arrowhead? Called firestones, or flint. Stone Age people rub firestones together. Make spark. Make fire."

Andrew picked up tiny chips of the firestones and put them in his pocket. "These could come in handy," he said.

Whoosh . . . whoosh . . . came a soft sound in the silent place.

Andrew turned his light up. "Oh, it's just a bat," he said.

meep . . . "Vampire bat!" squeaked Thudd.

WEIRD-A-MUNDO!

"Eeuuw!" said Judy, running to get under the bug skeleton. "You said there were no vampire bats here, Thudd!"

meep . . . "Sometimes animal move to new place," said Thudd. "Maybe vampire bat get lost."

"And now it's looking for blood!" said Judy. "Well, it's not going to get mine!"

Just as Andrew and Judy flopped the skeleton over themselves, the vampire bat swooped low.

"I've always wanted to see a vampire bat," said Andrew. He lifted the skeleton just a crack.

"Leaping lizards!" he cried. "This guy should be the star of his own horror movie!"

meep . . . "Vampire bat got nose that feel heat from animal," said Thudd. "Nose help bat find good place to suck blood, too.

"But Drewd and Oody not gotta worry. Vampire bat suck blood from sleeping animal."

"Then let's move it!" said Judy. "I don't want that bozo-bat to think we're snoozing!"

"It's headed back toward where we came from," said Andrew, peeking out.

meep . . . "Maybe suck blood from other bats," said Thudd.

Andrew spied a narrow space between two of the mammoth tusks. They crept through it and kept hiking toward the glow of light.

As they scrambled around a bend in the rock wall, the glow got brighter. They could see it through the bug skeleton.

plip . . . plip . . . plip . . . came the soft sound of water dripping.

Andrew lifted the skeleton.

At first all Andrew could see was a glowing, twinkly blur. Then his eyes got used to the light.

"Holy moly!" he said.

They were in an enormous room. It was as long as two football fields and as high as a ten-story building.

Huge shapes hung from the ceiling and rose from the floor. Many looked like enormous glistening white icicles. Others were shaped like waterfalls. Some looked like twisty tree branches and wedding cakes and strange animals.

"Weird-a-mundo!" said Judy.

"Looks like an ice palace!" said Andrew.

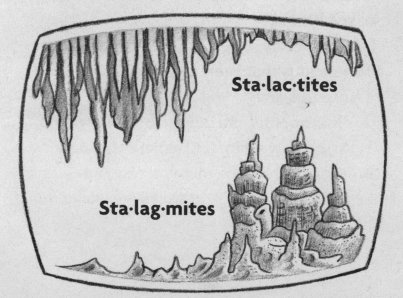

meep . . . "Shapes hanging from ceiling called stalactites," said Thudd. "Shapes coming up from floor called stalagmites."

Thudd pointed to his face screen.

"Water dripping from cave ceiling carry special stony stuff," said Thudd. "Kinda like stuff teeth made of. Every water drop leave tiny bit of stony stuff behind. Stony stuff build up. Make stalactite. Make stalagmite. Take hundred years for stalactite to grow one inch!"

plip . . . *plip* . . . *plip* . . .

A drop of water sloshed over Andrew and soaked him.

Everywhere, water was dripping, making little streams that came together and trickled off into the cave.

"It's brighter up ahead," Andrew said. "Let's see if we can find where the light is coming from. Maybe there's a way out."

Judy kicked the bottom of a stalagmite.

"We're just getting deeper and deeper into this stupid cave," she said.

meep . . . "Follow water. Find way out."

Judy rolled her eyes and picked up her side of the bug skeleton. Andrew and Judy crept over the slippery stones near a stream.

Suddenly the glow became a bright beam from high up. Andrew looked up. There was a hole in the cave ceiling! Andrew could see the moon!

"Wowzers schnauzers!" said Andrew. *"That's* where the light is coming from!"

"Hey!" said Judy. "Maybe we can climb a stalactite and get out of here."

"Noop! Noop! Noop!" said Thudd. "Stalactite slippery, slippery, slippery! Gotta follow water!"

Hauling the bug skeleton between them, Andrew and Judy trudged on.

Suddenly Andrew slipped. "Urf!" he cried as he slid down a large, bumpy boulder.

Andrew landed on his back in an ice-cold stream. The boulder loomed above him. At its top were two large, round holes. There was a triangle-shaped hole in the middle—and teeth at the bottom!

"Uh-oh," he said. "It's a . . . a . . . *skull!*"

GOOD-BYE TO THE STONE AGE

"Eeeeeuuuw!" said Judy, looking down from the top.

Andrew crept to the edge of the stream. Judy shoved the bug skeleton down to him, then slid down herself.

They looked up at the skull.

"I wonder what happened to this person," said Judy.

meep . . . "This could be burial place," said Thudd. "In Stone Age, humans bring dead to cave. Sometimes bring just bones.

"Look!" Thudd pointed to a round shape next to the skull. "Little jar," he said. "Maybe food inside. Gift for dead person."

"I wonder what this person's life was like," said Andrew.

Judy looked farther down the stream. "Cheese Louise!" she exclaimed. "There's another skull!"

"Thudd is right," said Andrew. "This must have been a burial place."

"Or a very bad Stone Age camping trip," said Judy. "Let's get out of here."

Andrew looked at the stream and the cockroach skeleton and scratched his ear. "Woofers!" he shouted. "The stream is pretty wide here. We could use the bug skeleton as a boat!"

"We don't have paddles," said Judy. "We won't be able to steer."

meep . . . "Not need paddles," said Thudd. "Stream go fast. Carry Drewd and Oody to end of cave."

"Humph," said Judy. "Anything to get past these spooky bones *fast*."

Andrew flipped the bug skeleton over. The crack was on top and the legs dangled down. Andrew dragged the skeleton into the icy stream and held it steady while Judy scrambled into the back. Then Andrew climbed into the front, almost tipping their strange boat.

The bug boat wobbled as it took off down the stream.

"I'm closing my eyes," said Judy. "Tell me when we're past the skulls."

"Okey-dokey!" said Thudd.

But Andrew couldn't take his eyes off the skulls as their boat passed by.

These people went to sleep knowing that a saber-toothed tiger could come into their cave, thought Andrew.

I wonder if they were happy. Imagine living without flushing toilets and pizza!

The stream got wider and wilder as other streams rushed into it.

Ahead was the entrance to a tunnel. It looked like a huge, dark, yawning mouth with pointy stalactites for teeth.

They passed under the scary-looking stalactite teeth and into the darkness.

WORMS, BEAUTIFUL WORMS

meep . . . "Can open eyes now, Oody," said Thudd.

They were in a dark, narrow, rocky tunnel. A strong current was speeding them along.

The tunnel was getting wider and higher. Ahead, patches of light danced on the water.

The stream dragged them around a bend and into another enormous room of the cave. The stalactites above twinkled with blue-green lights.

"Jumping gerbils!" said Andrew. "Looks like someone put holiday decorations on the stalactites!"

meep . . . "Glowworms!" said Thudd. "Glowworm is kind of baby insect.

"Glowworm make silk thread, like spider. Sticky! Sticky! Sticky! Hang thread from top of cave.

"Mosquitoes, other bugs fly to light of glowworm. Fly through sticky threads. Get caught! Glowworm crawl down thread and eat prey."

"Sheesh," Judy grumbled, slapping her

hand on the side of the boat. "Everybody's always eating some— Youch!" she cried. "Something bit my hand!"

Andrew looked down into the clear water. Fish the size of fingers were darting everywhere!

"Leaping lizards!" said Andrew. "Look at all these fish! And they're all white! And there's one of those white salamanders we were following!"

meep . . . "Lotsa cave animals got no color. Color not help animal here cuz everything dark, everything blind.

"Animal with color need more food than animal that not got color. Animal that not got color live longer here than animal with color."

"Strange-a-mundo!" said Judy.

Ahead of them, a rocky ledge jutted out in the stream. The bug boat was speeding toward it.

"Hang on, Judy!" said Andrew. "We're gonna crash!"

Plumph . . .

It was a soft crash.

"Whew!" said Andrew. "That was like hitting a pillow!"

Andrew reached out to push the boat off the ledge. Instead of touching rock, his hands touched something soft.

"This stuff feels like cotton candy!" he said.

When Andrew tried to pull his hands away, he couldn't!

He tugged. Then he yanked.

"What are you *doing,* Andrew?" asked Judy.

"Um, this stuff is really sticky," said Andrew. "I'm kind of super stuck."

meep . . . "Glowworm web!" said Thudd. "Web fall from top of cave!"

"Judy," said Andrew. "Grab my belt. When I count to three, give me a big jerk."

"You already *are* a big jerk!" said Judy.

"One, two, three!" said Andrew.

Judy jerked. Andrew came loose and fell into the bottom of the bug boat. The boat teetered and water slopped in.

"You know," said Andrew, "this glow-worm web is really neat stuff. Maybe I can use it in one of my inventions."

"Don't you dare touch that stuff again, Bug-Brain," said Judy.

"I won't touch it," said Andrew.

He leaned over the side of the bug boat and grabbed a hollow cockroach leg. He bent it from side to side and twisted it until it came loose.

"Woofers!" said Andrew. "This leg is heavy!"

He shoved the cockroach leg into the glob of glowworm web. He spun the leg around till he had collected a big glob of web. Then he tossed it into the bottom of the bug boat.

Andrew snapped off another cockroach

leg and used the tip of it to push them away from the ledge.

The tiny boat lurched into the stream again. It bounced and dipped as fish and salamanders snapped at it.

A fish's head popped up so close to Andrew, he could have kissed its fishy lips.

"Holy moly!" said Andrew. "These guys *don't have eyes*!"

meep . . . "Cave fish and cave salamander born with eyes," said Thudd. "Then skin grow over eyes. Eyes sink into head."

"That's *disgusting*!" said Judy.

"Cave animals not need eyes in cave that got no light. Cave animals find prey by smell. Feel prey move.

"Easy for eyes to get hurt, too," Thudd continued. "Easier for cave animal that not got eyes to survive here than animal that got eyes!"

The ceiling of the glowworm cave dipped low. The river was moving frighteningly fast. Ahead loomed the entrance to a dark tunnel.

As the bug boat swirled into the blackness, Andrew noticed that the beam of the flashlight was very dim. He could barely see the water.

Must be the batteries, thought Andrew. The beam began to flicker—and then it went out.

THE LIGHT AT THE END OF THE TUNNEL

The river dragged them through the cold darkness.

"Cheese Louise!" said Judy. "Put on your flashlight, Andrew! There could be a humongous waterfall ahead and we wouldn't even know it!"

"Um, I think the batteries are dead," said Andrew. He was silent for a moment. "But maybe the Stone Age people can save us."

"Huh?" said Judy.

"I picked up pieces of their firestones," said Andrew. "I can use them to light a fire."

"We don't have anything to burn," said Judy.

"We can use the bug leg with the glow-worm web as a torch," said Andrew. He picked it up off the bottom of the bug boat and passed it back to Judy. "Hang on to this," he said.

"Not a bad idea, Bug-Brain," said Judy. She waved her hands in the darkness until she felt the bug leg and grabbed it.

Andrew pulled the tiny firestones out of his pocket.

meep . . . "Gotta hit one stone against other stone," said Thudd.

Andrew slammed one piece against the other. Nothing happened. He smashed them together hard. Still nothing. He kept on trying.

Suddenly a few tiny flashes of yellow-orange light curved into the air.

"Woo-hoo!" yelled Andrew. "We've got sparks!"

Andrew felt around and took the bug leg from Judy. He braced it between his knees, then smacked the stones hard. Sparks flew high!

Ffffft . . . WHOOOOSH!

A ball of fire bigger than a beach ball leapt up from the water!

"AAAAAAAAAH!" screamed Judy.

"YEOOOOW!" hollered Andrew, jumping as though a Tyrannosaurus had come up behind him. Quick as a lightning flash, the ball of fire disappeared. But the torch was lit!

"What was *that*?" asked Judy.

meep . . . "Like swamp fire," said Thudd. "Gas come up from under ground."

"Woofers!" said Andrew. "This torch seems kind of dangerous, but it will keep away the salamanders."

meep . . . "Fish, too," said Thudd.

"And we can see where we're going," said Judy.

They sat silently as the boat bobbed along. Andrew was thinking how good the heat of the torch felt when he saw a lump rising ahead of them. A rock was sticking out of the water and they were speeding straight at it!

Klick!

Their bug boat slammed into the rock. Water sloshed over the sides of the boat and soaked the Dubbles.

ch . . . ch . . . ch . . . Judy shivered. "The water's *so cold.*"

"Hold the torch," said Andrew to Judy. "I'll get us out of here."

Andrew picked up the other bug leg and used it to push them off the rock and back into the river.

The river was getting faster and rougher. And Andrew could see more rocks sticking up ahead.

meep . . . "When river got lotsa big rocks," said Thudd, "water go fast, fast, fast around rocks. Places in river that got lotsa rocks and fast water called rapids."

As Andrew scanned the river for rocks, he thought he saw something else. He squinted. *Am I seeing spots?* he thought. *Or is that a dot of light out there?*

But the dot was getting bigger and brighter.

"There's light ahead!" said Andrew.

"Humph," Judy grumped. "Probably just some more stupid glowworms."

But soon they could see the craggy opening. Through it they could see the rising sun!

TAKING THE WRONG TERN

"We made it!" cheered Andrew.

"I don't believe it!" said Judy. "Thudd was right!"

"Thunkoo, Oody," said Thudd. His face screen turned pink.

Andrew used the bug leg to keep the boat from smacking into boulders.

With the light from the cave opening, they didn't need the torch anymore. Judy dunked it in the river and used it to push them away from the rocks.

At last they swirled through the opening of the cave. The light was so bright, it hurt their eyes.

"Where are we?" said Judy, blinking at the land around them.

On both sides of the river stretched fields of weeds. In the distance was a pine tree forest.

"I saw a rusty plow on the riverbank," said Andrew. "Maybe this is a farm. Maybe we can find someone who can get us back to school. But first we have to get to the riverbank."

"There's lots of weeds hanging into the water," said Judy. "If we get near them, we can grab on and pull ourselves to shore."

Andrew and Judy used their bug legs like hooks.

"Got one!" said Judy. Her bug leg had caught on a vine trailing in the current.

"Yay, Oody!" said Thudd.

"Super-duper pooper-scooper!" said Andrew.

As Judy held the boat in place, Andrew climbed onto the vine and pulled himself toward the shore. Judy climbed out and followed. The bug boat took off down the river.

In a minute, Andrew and Judy arrived onshore at the end of the vine.

"Woofers!" said Andrew, leaning against a big brown lump. It was hard, but not as hard as a rock, and the vine was growing out of it.

"I landed on a potato!" said Andrew. "I see one of its eyes!"

"Who cares about your stupid potato, Bug-Brain," said Judy. "We're in a field. There are mice in fields—and *snakes*. We could get *eaten*. We need to get out of here—*fast*."

"I know how to make a battery out of a potato!" said Andrew. "If we had some electricity, maybe I could get us back to normal size! Or at least a little bigger. We'd be able to get back to school and get totally unshrunk!

"Do you have anything that's made out of metal, Judy?"

"Maybe some hairpins," said Judy,

running her fingers through her soggy, tangled hair. She pulled out six hairpins and a hair clip and handed them to Andrew.

A shadow darkened the ground.

Andrew looked up to see the white underside of a bird overhead. It was flying low and unsteadily.

"That bird is coming in for a landing," said Andrew.

"Hide!" said Judy. "Birds eat bugs, and we're looking awfully buggy!"

meep . . . "Hide in skunk cabbage," said Thudd, pointing to a strange plant behind Judy. Its single reddish leaf was twisted into a round tent shape. There was a slit on its side.

"Pee-yew!" said Judy as they rushed toward the skunk cabbage.

They crept inside the slit.

"It's warm here!" said Andrew.

"Yoop! Yoop! Yoop!" said Thudd. "Plant make heat."

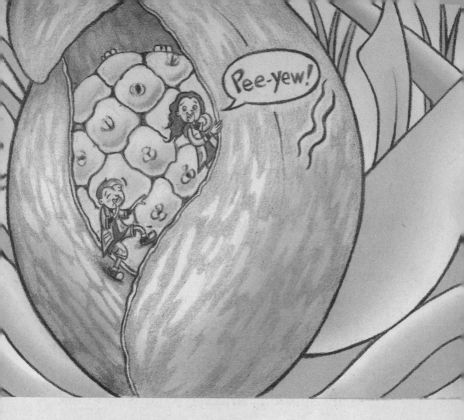

They peeked out of the slit. The bird landed on the edge of the river and began to drink. A long feather drooped from one of its wings.

meep . . . "Bird is arctic tern," said Thudd. "Arctic tern make long, long flight, from North Pole to South Pole and then back again, every year. Called migration.

"Most time, arctic tern not stop between Arctic and Antarctic. This bird got problem with flight feather."

The bird finished drinking. It hopped into the air, flapped its wings—and fell back to the ground. Then it walked toward a patch of grass and tucked its head under a wing.

"Aw," said Judy. "The poor thing. I wonder if we can help."

meep . . . "Maybe if feather get stuck back in place," said Thudd.

"Let's sneak up and see what we can do," said Judy.

They left the skunk cabbage and crept up to the bird. It didn't seem to notice them.

"Let's climb up on the wing," said Judy. "Maybe we can tuck the feather in place with my hairpins."

"Let's try it," said Andrew.

They climbed onto the wing and crept

among the feathers. Andrew tugged at the long, heavy flight feather but hardly moved it.

"Give me a hand here, Judy," he said. She grabbed the feather, too.

"One . . . two . . . three!" said Andrew, taking a deep breath. *"Oomph!"*

Together Andrew and Judy pulled with all their might and hauled the feather up to the other flight feathers. Judy tucked the feather in place with her hairpins and clip.

"Okay," said Judy. "Let go of the feather. We'll see if it holds."

Andrew let go. The feather stayed in place.

"Super-duper pooper-scooper!" he shouted.

The bird suddenly shook itself and stretched both wings!

Andrew and Judy were tossed onto the bird's back. The arctic tern hopped into the air and flapped. She was off!

"YAAAAAAH!" screamed Judy as they rose into the air.

"Hang on!" yelled Andrew, clinging to a feather.

"We're going for a ride!"

TO BE CONTINUED IN ANDREW, JUDY, AND THUDD'S

NEXT EXCITING ADVENTURE:

ANDREW LOST
IN THE JUNGLE!

In stores January 2007

THUDD

TRUE STUFF

Thudd wanted to tell you more about bats and caves, but he was busy keeping Andrew and Judy from being chewed by beetles and chomped by salamanders. Here's what he wanted to say:

• Mosquitoes suck your blood to make food for their babies. Only female mosquitoes bite. A mosquito can drink four times her own weight in blood!

    Male mosquitoes are peaceful little guys. They stick to drinking nectar from flowers.

• Mosquitoes' antennas feel the heat of living creatures. They also sense the water and a gas in the air that animals breathe out. That's how they find a living creature to bite.

Mosquito repellents keep the antennas from being able to find what they're looking for.

• The nasty whine of a mosquito comes from the beating of its wings. The sound is annoying to us, but it's music to the sensitive antennas of a male mosquito. When he hears that special *nyeeeeee*, he knows there's a lovely female mosquito—maybe a mate—nearby.

• Some moths have a super way of protecting themselves from being eaten by birds—they look like bird poop!

• The smallest bat is the bumblebee bat. It's about an inch long and weighs less than a penny. This little fellow is also the smallest mammal.

The largest bat is the giant flying fox. This guy's wings stretch almost six feet from tip to tip, but he weighs only about two pounds.

• In total darkness, bats use sound waves to "see" wires as thin as a human hair!

• Baby bats' claws are so sharp, they can hang on to something as smooth as a lightbulb.

• More than 20 million bats live in Bracken Cave in Texas. Each night, these bats eat a quantity of insects that weighs as much as sixty-three elephants!

• In some places, people are afraid of bats. They have even blown up the caves where bats roost. But if you don't want to get bitten by mosquitoes and other insect pests, help protect the bats!

• Vampire bats drink only about a tablespoon of blood each night. They don't suck blood. Their sharp teeth cut the skin of an animal— usually a cow or a bird—and then they lick up the blood. Their saliva keeps blood from clotting, so they can lap up blood for hours!

• When an underground space has many "rooms," scientists call it a cavern. When there's just one big space, it's called a cave. In this book, Andrew, Judy, and Thudd visit a cavern—it has different "rooms." But Thudd didn't bother to point out the difference.

• Cave rock is made up mostly of calcium, the same stuff shells and teeth and bones are made of. Cave rock came from the shells of sea creatures. After they died, their shells got buried and squashed into stone. Sometimes this stone is pushed up to the surface of the earth by the same geologic forces that slowly move the continents.

• You can do an easy experiment to see how calcium can be washed away. Put an egg in a glass and cover the egg with vinegar. The eggshell is made mostly of calcium, like cave rock. The vinegar is like the water that drips through the rock into the cave.

Put the glass in the refrigerator and check the egg every day. Lift it very gently with a large spoon and touch it. What happens to the eggshell? How long does it take? Try the same experiment with Coca-Cola!!

WHERE TO FIND MORE TRUE STUFF

Would you like to find out more about the batty creatures of the night? Here are some books you might enjoy:

• *Billions of Bats* by Miriam Schlein (Hagerstown, MD: Lippincott Williams & Wilkins, 1982). Lots of great information about some of the most interesting bats, including the vampires!

• *Zipping, Zapping, Zooming Bats* by Ann Earle (New York: HarperTrophy, 1995). All about bats: how they fly, feed, hibernate, take care of themselves and each other—and how we can take care of them.

- *Amazing Bats* by Frank Greenaway (New York: Knopf Books for Young Readers, 1991). Do you want to impress your friends and parents with bat facts? Read this book!
- *Bat Loves the Night* by Nicola Davies (Cambridge, MA: Candlewick Press, 2004). This terrific book gives you a feeling for a day in the life of a bat.

Turn the page
for a sneak peek at
Andrew, Judy, and Thudd's
next exciting adventure—

ANDREW LOST IN THE JUNGLE!

Available January 2007

IT'S A JUNGLE DOWN THERE

Andrew Dubble poked his head above the feathers on the bird's back. A cold wind smacked his face as he peered at the earth far below.

"I see land!" Andrew shouted. "It looks green down there!"

Another feather on the bird's back twitched and a pile of frizzy dark hair popped up. It was Judy.

"But this bird is an arctic tern!" said Judy, tugging her hair away from her face. "It's not going to land in some nice green place. These birds fly from the North Pole to the South Pole—to *Antarctica*!"

meep . . . "Maybe bird need rest," came a squeaky voice from Andrew's shirt pocket. It was Andrew's mini-robot and best friend, Thudd.

The bird spread its wings and glided down. The land was getting closer. Andrew could see a sandy shore and a forest beyond.

"Looks like a deserted island," said Andrew.

"Noop! Noop! Noop!" said Thudd. "Australia!"

Now the bird was swooping over the forest. It looked like a bumpy blanket of green. Here and there, tall trees poked up.

The bird flew down into the trees.

Andrew blinked as his eyes got used to the dim light.

Judy craned her neck. "Look at this place!" she said. "A tangle of trees and vines! It's a *jungle*!"

meep . . . "Rain forest," said Thudd. "Australian rain forest. Strangest place on earth. Got plants and animals that not live any other place. Got eighty-six thousand kindsa insects! Got ten thousand kindsa spiders! Got most poisonous snakes in world!"

Judy groaned.

Their bird slowed down and settled itself on a branch.

"Oof!" gasped Judy, lunging forward when the bird stopped.

"Wowzers!" hollered Andrew.

meep . . . "Gotta get off arctic tern," said Thudd. "Bird can fly off soon."

"Yeah," said Judy. "Her next stop is penguin country. *Brrrrr!*"

Andrew pulled himself down to the long flight feathers near the edge of the tern's wing.

Just then, the bird swiveled her head. Andrew saw himself reflected in a shiny black eye.

He ducked under a long flight feather and

pulled it down tightly over himself.

"Judy!" hollered Andrew. "Climb down to the edge of the wing and jump to the branch. You can make it!"

A pointy red beak plunged down close to Andrew. It grabbed the bottom of one of the feathers and nibbled along it right up to the tip.

meep . . . "Bird preen feather," said Thudd. "Make feather smooth for flying. Get rid of little bugs."

The beak preened another feather even closer to Andrew.

"Wowzers schnauzers!" said Andrew. "We've got to get out of here!"

Just then, the red beak grabbed the feather Andrew was clinging to and began to preen it. The beak pushed him to the very tip of the feather. He could barely hang on. That black eye was looking right at him.

She's hungry after such a long flight, and I'm bug-sized, thought Andrew. He let go.